This Book Belongs To:

....

Illustrated by Caroline Pedler

Retold by Gaby Goldsack

This edition published by Parragon in 2012 for Index Books, Ltd

Parragon
Chartist House
15-17 Trim Street
Bath BA1 1HA, UK
www.parragon.com

Copyright © Parragon Books Ltd 2001

ISBN 978-1-78186-225-4
Printed in China

A Letter to Santa

Bath · New York · Singapore · Hong Kong · Cologne · Delhi
Melbourne · Amsterdam · Johannesburg · Shenzhen

On Christmas Eve, when the snow was all white,
I sat on the floor with a letter to write.
Before I began, I thought what to say
I'd like Santa to leave for me on Christmas day.

Dear Santa,

(I neatly wrote)
I hope you are well
when you read this note.
I'm sure you have noticed
that I have been good,
just as my mummy
told me I should.
So if it's alright,
for Christmas I'd like –
a book or a train set
or maybe a bike.

Then when I'd finished, I printed my name,
and added kisses again and again.

Across to the fireplace I boldly went,
and up the chimney my letter was sent.
For that is the place, I'm sure you will know,
that letters to Santa should always go.
Just how they get there, I don't understand,
but that is the way to Santa's cold land.

That winter's night when the world was asleep,
I snuggled in bed – not a sound, not a peep –
thinking of Santa and the toys he would bring,
and the fun I would have on Christmas morning.
When, all of a sudden, where could I be?
Out in the snow in a strange country!

Next to a cabin in the deep crispy snow,
I shiver with cold as I peer in the window.
It's Santa's workshop! I must creep inside.
No one will see me if I'm careful to hide.
Sssh! I must be quiet as I tiptoe in,
to see where our Christmas toys all begin.

I can see Santa reading letters galore.
Hey, he's got mine, by his feet, on the floor!
A map of the world is pinned to the wall,
showing Santa the way to the homes of us all,
with rooftop instructions so there is no doubt,
that any small child is ever left out.

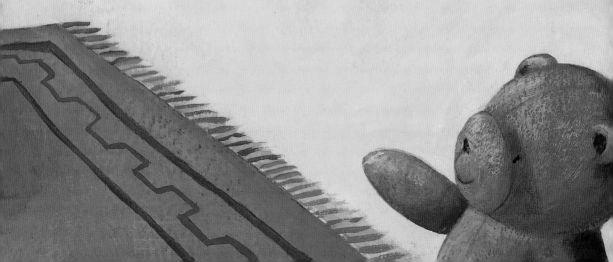

Just see how busy all Santa's elves are:
One's making a doll's house, one a toy car;
another elf's painting a wonderful train,

and this elf is putting the wings on a plane.
Look at that little elf riding a bike,
It's just like the one I said I would like.

This must be the room where presents are packed.
They're measured for size, then carefully wrapped.
Tied up with ribbons and finished with bows,
each with a name tag so Santa Claus knows.
Wherever you look there's bustle and scurry.
Everyone seems in a terrible hurry.

Here are the elves who help Santa get dressed.
There's Santa's coat and hat, all neatly pressed.
And there are his boots getting a shine.
They look so smart, I wish they were mine.
I think this room is as good as the rest,
for it's the place that makes Santa look best.

Back in the workshop, the parcel track halts.
It seems there's a problem with one of its bolts.
The elves are worried – there's trouble in the air.
But here comes Santa to make the repair.
In no time at all, parcels speed on their way,
out to the stables and onto the sleigh.

Outside the stable, the reindeer wait.
I count them all up and, yes, there are eight!
Their hooves are polished, their bells burnished bright,
as elves brush and groom them in the moonlight.
Their harnesses gleam, their coats all shine.
Now the reindeer are restless, as it's almost time!

The sleigh is now packed and the reindeer ready.
Santa at the reins cries, "Away now, go steady!"
High over clouds and hills they fly,
galloping onwards across the sky.
Soon, beneath them, rooftops they see
where inside asleep are children like me!

When I wake up, it's Christmas Day,
and just like my dream, Santa's been! Hooray!
My stocking is filled up with candy cane,
And I'm sure in that parcel there must be a train.
Great! There's a bicycle propped by my bed.
My letter to Santa must have been read!

HOPSCOTCH

Naughty Nancy

First published in 2002 by
Franklin Watts
96 Leonard Street
London
EC2A 4XD

Franklin Watts Australia
56 O'Riordan Street
Alexandria
NSW 2015

A CIP catalogue record for this book is available
from the British Library.

ISBN 0 7496 4476 1 (hbk)
ISBN 0 7496 4622 5 (pbk)

Series Editor: Louise John
Series Advisor: Dr Barrie Wade
Cover Design: Jason Anscomb
Design: Peter Scoulding

Printed in Hong Kong

HOPSCOTCH

Naughty
Nancy

by Anne Cassidy and Desideria Guicciardini

W
FRANKLIN WATTS
LONDON•SYDNEY

Norman had to look after his little sister, Nancy. She was the naughtiest girl he knew.

"I'm going out now," said Mum.
"Don't let Nancy frighten the sheep,
upset the hens, or worry the pigs!"

"Make sure she doesn't get into trouble and try to keep her clothes clean!" she added.

Norman was not happy.

Norman took Nancy outside into the garden. He showed her the trees and the flowers.

"Look at this pretty, red rose, Nancy," he said.

But Nancy was already chasing
the hens.

"No!" shouted Norman. He ran into the hen house after Nancy and caught her just in time.

Norman took Nancy to see the fishpond. He showed her the goldfish and the slimy frogs.

But Nancy wasn't looking.

She was trying to jump across the
stepping stones to the other side.

"No!" shouted Norman, splashing into the water.

Norman caught Nancy just in time.

He also caught some fish and a
slimy frog!

Norman was wet and fed up. "Let's go into the sunshine and play hide-and-seek in the meadow," he said to Nancy.

Norman counted slowly to one hundred. But Nancy wasn't playing.

Nancy was trying to count
the sheep. The sheep weren't
pleased at all.

Norman ran after Nancy and tried
to catch her. But he just got in the
way!

Norman took Nancy for a long walk in the woods. He took his nature book with him and showed her a beautiful, blue butterfly. But Nancy wasn't looking.

21

Nancy wanted to catch her own butterfly and climbed up a tree.

"No!" shouted Norman and climbed up the tree after her.

But Nancy had jumped down.

Norman wasn't so lucky.

The branch broke, he fell to the
ground and landed in a bush!

On the way home, Norman and
Nancy passed the pig huts.
Nancy wanted to look inside.
She opened the gate.

Norman tried to close the gate
but, too late, the pigs came
trotting out!

They pushed past Norman and he
fell in the mud.

"I've had enough!" shouted
Norman. "We're going straight
home."

And he marched Nancy back
to the house.

Mum was very pleased.

"What a good girl you are, Nancy.
Your clothes are clean and your
hair is tidy."

"What a shame about your brother!" she added.

"In future, I think I'll call him naughty Norman!"

Hopscotch has been specially designed to fit the requirements of the National Literacy Strategy. It offers real books by top authors and illustrators for children developing their reading skills.

There are five other Hopscotch stories to choose from:

Marvin, the Blue Pig

Written by Karen Wallace, illustrated by Lisa Williams

Marvin is the only blue pig on the farm. He tries hard to make himself pink but nothing seems to work. Then, one day, his friend Esther gives him some advice...

Plip and Plop

Written by Penny Dolan, illustrated by Lisa Smith

Plip and Plop are two pesky pigeons that live in Sam's grandpa's garden. And if anyone went out, Plip and Plop got busy... Sam has to think of a way to get rid of them!

The Queen's Dragon

Written by Anne Cassidy, illustrated by Gwyneth Williamson

The Queen is fed up with her dragon, Harry. His wings are floppy and his fire has gone out! She decides to find a new one, but it's not quite as easy as she thinks...

Flora McQuack

Written by Penny Dolan, illustrated by Kay Widdowson

Flora McQuack finds a lost egg by the side of the loch and decides to hatch it. But when the egg cracks open, Flora is in for a surprise!

Willie the Whale

Written by Joy Oades, illustrated by Barbara Vagnozzi

Willie the Whale decides to go on a round-the-world adventure – from the South Pole to the desert and even to New York. But is the city really the place for a big, friendly whale?